THIS BOOK BELONGS TO

Adele Woodbury

from Nan Nan
& Poppy '86

A LITTLE OWL BOOK

THE GINGERBREAD MAN

retold by Hilda Young
illustrated by Jane Cunningham

WORLD

There was once a little old man and a little old woman who lived in a tiny house at the top of a very steep hill. The little old man worked hard in the garden growing fruit and vegetables and looking after his hens, and the little old woman kept the house neat and tidy, and baked lots of lovely things to eat.

One day the little old woman decided to make something
rather special for her husband, who was very fond of his
wife's cooking.

"I'll make him a gingerbread man," she said. "I know he'll
like that."

The little old woman got out her cookery book and set to
work.

She shaped out the gingerbread man with her clever fingers, giving him two raisin eyes, a tiny currant nose, a smiling cherry mouth and then she put some little sweets as buttons on his jacket.

"What a handsome little gingerbread man you are!" she cried, as she popped him in the oven to bake.

"My, that gingerbread smells good," said the little old man coming into the kitchen a short time later. "Is it ready?"

"I'll just look and see," replied the old woman, thinking what a lovely surprise her husband would get when he saw the gingerbread man.

The little old woman opened the oven door ... and what a surprise *she* got! The golden brown gingerbread man was lying on the baking tray, baked to perfection. He looked up at the little old woman, smiling at her with his red cherry mouth ... and then he gave the old woman a big wink! Yes, he really did!

"Oh my goodness!" cried the little old woman. "Husband, did you see that?"

But before the little old man could reply, the gingerbread man jumped out of the oven and ran across the kitchen towards the open door.

"Come back, come back!" cried the little old woman. She ran after the gingerbread man as fast as her plump little legs would carry her.

But the gingerbread man would not stop. As he ran he called out:

"Run, run, as fast as you can!
You can't catch me, I'm the gingerbread man!"

"Stop, stop, I say!" ordered the little old man, chasing after the gingerbread man as he raced down the garden path, scattering the chickens who rushed to get out of the way.

But the gingerbread man only laughed as he called:

"Run, run, as fast as you can!

You can't catch me, I'm the gingerbread man!"

The gingerbread man ran off down the hill, followed by the old man and his wife. The gingerbread man ran on until he came to a boy and girl playing leap frog in the sun.

"Look, a gingerbread man!" cried the boy in delight.

"Stop, we *love* gingerbread men!" pleaded the little girl.

The gingerbread man just laughed . . . and the children tried to catch him.

But although the boy and his sister ran very fast, they could not catch the gingerbread man. As they chased after him, he called out:

"Run, run, as fast as you can!
You can't catch me, I'm the gingerbread man!
I'm running away from the little old woman,
And the little old man!
And I can run away from you,
I can, can, can!"

And he could, too, because . . .
the little old woman . . .
the little old man . . .
and the boy
and his sister
just could not catch the gingerbread man!

Next the gingerbread man passed a pretty little black kitten sitting on a fence.

"Stop, stop, meow, stop right no-ow!" meowed the little black kitten. "I like gingerbread men!"

And the little black kitten jumped down from the fence and started to chase the gingerbread man.

But the gingerbread man just laughed and laughed as he shouted:

"Run, run, as fast as you can!
You can't catch me, I'm the gingerbread man!
I've outrun a little old woman,
And a little old man!
A little boy, and his sister, too!
And I certainly can outrun you!"

And away ran the gingerbread man followed by the little old woman, the little old man, the boy and his sister and the pretty little black kitten.

Soon the gingerbread man passed a brown and white cow grazing in a green meadow.

"Stop, stop, please doo-oo!" mooed the cow.

But the gingerbread man just laughed at the cow.

As he jumped over a stile he called out:
"Run, run, as fast as you can!
I'm running away from a little old woman,
And a little old man!
And a boy and a girl and a kitten, too!
Why should I stop for someone like you?"

And, of course, the gingerbread man didn't stop, he just ran on and on and on, followed by the little old woman, the little old man, the little boy, the little girl, the little black kitten and the brown and white cow. But, oh dear me, they were all so very, very tired!

But suddenly the gingerbread man came to a swiftly flowing river, and for the first time since he ran out of the tiny house on the top of the steep hill, the gingerbread man stopped running.

There was no way he could cross that river by himself!

But just then a sly red fox popped out from behind a prickly blackberry bush. The fox smiled at the gingerbread man with his two rows of shiny, sharp teeth. "Hop onto my back, gingerbread man!" he cried. "I will take you safely across the river!"

"Thank you," replied the gingerbread man very politely.

The gingerbread man had seen the fox's sharp teeth, and so he did not climb onto the fox's back. Instead he sat on the tip of the fox's bushy tail, well away from those sharp teeth, and the fox started to swim across the river.

But as the fox swam on, the water rose higher and higher until it nearly covered the fox's bushy tail.

"If you don't hop onto my back now, you will get very wet!" called the fox to the gingerbread man.

So, very reluctantly, the gingerbread man jumped onto the fox's back.

But still the water rose higher and higher until soon it almost covered the fox's red back.

"Do hop onto my head, my dear gingerbread man," pleaded the fox. "I do not wish you to get wet!"

And so, watched by all the fishes in the river, the gingerbread man hopped onto the fox's head, clinging tightly to the fox's ears.

"Now I am quite safe!" thought the gingerbread man to himself. And he laughed aloud as he saw the old man, the old woman, the boy, the girl, the little black kitten and the brown and white cow looking at him from the river bank.

But the water still rose higher and higher until even the fox's ears began to get wet.

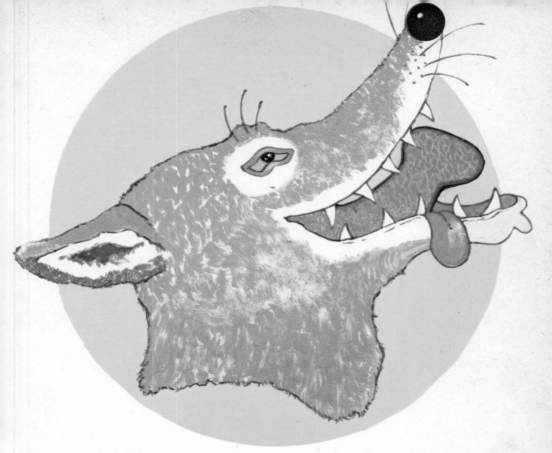

"Jump onto my nose, the water will never reach my nose!"
called the fox. "See, we have only a few more yards to go!"

The gingerbread man made a mighty hop . . . but he
never landed on the fox's nose!

Instead, the sly fox raised his head and . . .

Snip! Swallow! The red fox ate up the gingerbread man!
And that was the end of the gingerbread man!

Then the smart red fox swam to the other side of the river, shook his fur dry and disappeared into the trees, licking his lips.

"Never mind," said the old woman. "Everybody come home with me, and I'll make you all a gingerbread man of your very own!"

And she did!